Ice on Earth

Nicolas Brasch

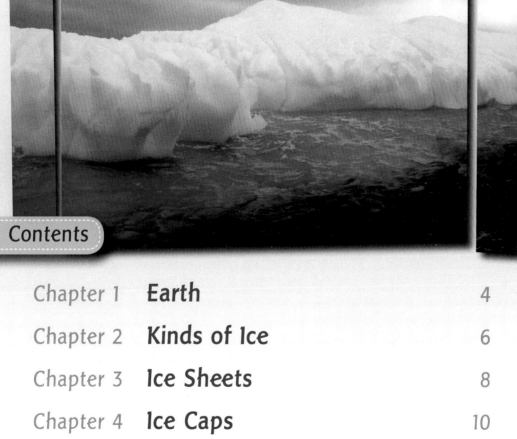

Contents

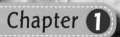

EARTH

This is Earth.
We live on Earth.
Earth is our home.

Earth

4

ice

rock

water

grass

Different things cover Earth.

Parts of Earth are covered by grass.
Parts of Earth are covered by rock.
Most of Earth is covered by water.
Some of this water is in the form
of ice.

KINDS OF ICE

There are different kinds of ice on Earth.

There are **ice sheets**, **ice caps** and **ice shelves**. There are also **icebergs** and **sea ice**.

ICE SHEETS

Ice sheets are the biggest kind of ice form on Earth.
Ice sheets are bigger than 50 000 **square kilometres**.

The biggest ice sheet on Earth covers Antarctica.
This ice sheet is bigger than 13 million square kilometres.
A lot of Earth's ice is in Antarctica.

Antarctica

Running Words 114

Chapter 4

ICE CAPS

Ice caps are like ice sheets.
But ice caps are smaller
than 50 000 square kilometres.

There are ice caps all over Earth.
Some people go to ice caps
and walk over them.
They do this for fun!

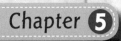

ICE SHELVES AND ICEBERGS

Ice shelves are big ice forms on land and on water.
Some of the ice shelf floats on water.
Some of the ice shelf is on land.

The Ross Ice Shelf in Antarctica is the biggest ice shelf on Earth. The Ross Ice Shelf is bigger than 500 000 square kilometres.

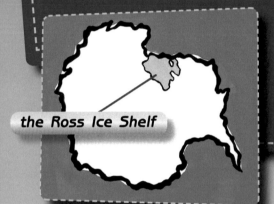

the Ross Ice Shelf

the Ross Ice Shelf

Icebergs are big lumps of ice that float in the sea.
Icebergs have come away from an ice sheet,
an ice cap or an ice shelf.

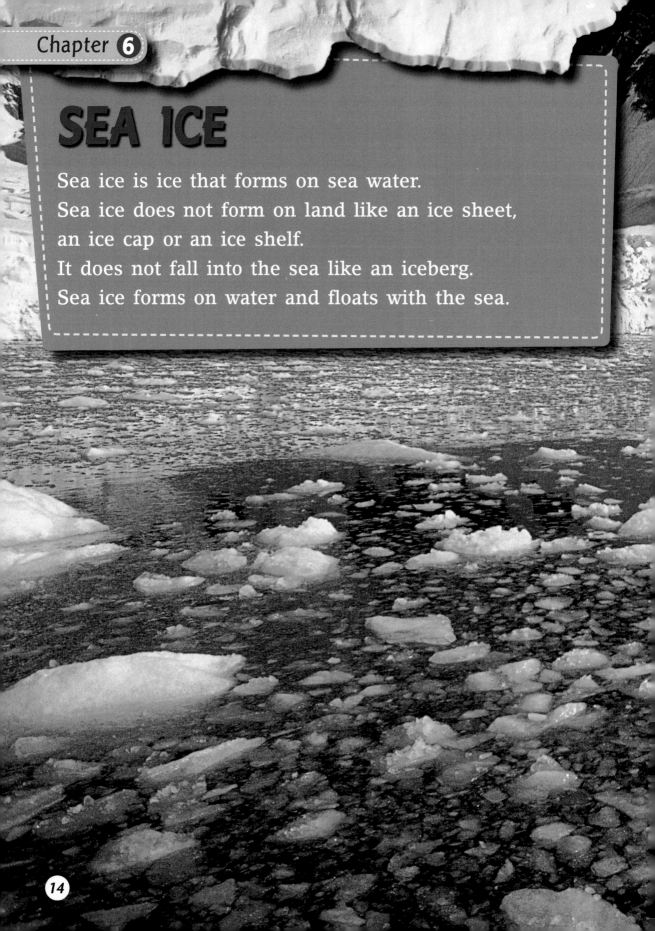

Chapter 6

SEA ICE

Sea ice is ice that forms on sea water.
Sea ice does not form on land like an ice sheet,
an ice cap or an ice shelf.
It does not fall into the sea like an iceberg.
Sea ice forms on water and floats with the sea.

Glossary

ice caps	ice sheets that cover an area smaller than 50 000 square kilometres
ice sheets	the biggest kind of ice form on Earth. Ice sheets cover areas bigger than 50 000 square kilometres.
ice shelves	very big forms of ice that are on land and on water
icebergs	big lumps of ice that float in the sea
sea ice	ice that forms on water
square kilometres	a unit of measurement showing the space of an area

Index